DOG ON TRIAL

(Based on a true event)

Joanna H. Kraus

ISBN 978-1-61225-474-6

Published by Mirror Publishing
Fort Payne, AL 35967
www.pagesofwonder.com

Printed in the USA

Acknowledgements

My appreciation and gratitude to the people who first introduced me to this landmark trial and helped facilitate my early research. They include the late Dr. William Hullfish, Arts for Children colleague, to Pat Kutz at the Lift Bridge Book Shop, to the staff at the Emily L. Knapp Museum in Brockport, New York and to my SUNY students who brought the story to life on stage.

Currently, I am extremely grateful to the East Bay Critique Group for their support, encouragement and suggestions as I worked on this chapter book. They are:Nancy Kors, Marleen Miller, Susan Nunes, Leslie Rupley, Sheryl Ruzek and Sally Tubach.

And, finally, my thanks to Chiara Savarese, who designed the dramatic cover illustration and to Neal Wooten, Managing Editor at Mirror Publishing, who made the book a reality.

Author's Note

This is a work of fiction, loosely based on Erie Canal history. However, all proper names have been changed in the interest of respecting the privacy of the individuals and canines involved. I first developed the material to be included as a scene for Our Spirit Shows, a celebration of the 1984 Rochester Sesquicentennial, by the Department of Theatre, School of Arts and Performance, College at Brockport State University of New York. Two years later, my participation play, The Shaggy Dog Murder Trial, toured area elementary schools. The full script was included in Beginnings in Literature (Scott, Foresman.) The play was published by Anchorage Press in 1988 and is now available through Dramatic Publishing.

Table of Contents

Chapter One
July 4th, 1936

July 4th promised fireworks and fried chicken.

We didn't suspect the danger looming, the disaster ahead.

Ma was rolling out pie dough on our oilcloth covered table and Dad was muttering as he read the newspaper, "A pound of butter jumps to thirty-nine cents."

"Land sakes, what's this world coming to," Mom exclaimed, then turned her attention to me. "Stop tormenting your oatmeal, Peter," as I picked out the raisins, which anybody knows is the good part. "Finish your breakfast," she continued. "I need you and Nick to pick me some strawberries. Mind you, that they're ripe," she said, as she lifted the dough onto the waiting pie dishes.

Dad winked, "And make sure they make it into the pie before you eat them." Mom's strawberry pie was famous, well as famous as a pie could be, in our canal village in upstate New York.

When I repeated my dad's instructions, Nick laughed,

handed me the remains of a buttermilk biscuit and then tossed a big fat juicy berry into his mouth. "I'm having it now instead of tonight," he said. Later, those words haunted me.

I remember my best friend's lean face, and the sun shining on his jet- black hair. Nick wanted to ride African elephants and climb the tallest tree in the Amazon rain forest. He did not want to spend the rest of his life working in his pa's grocery store.

"Wouldn't ever go hungry," I said.

"Not gonna spend the rest of my life counting cans of tuna fish," he scoffed.

"You'd always have plenty of bubble gum. Wouldn't have to sneak it."

Nick grinned and pulled two pieces from his pocket. "Ready?" he asked and challenged me to see who could blow the biggest bubble.

Though we were both twelve, I was shorter, skinnier, and while Nick longed for real adventures, I liked mine in comic books.

Last winter when the canal froze over, Nick didn't bother to test the thickness of the ice as we started to slide across. But when the ice cracked under my feet, he yanked me away. "Too cold for a swim," he joked. That's when I began to think about what my dad calls "consequences."

I told Nick that when my great-great grandfather was our age he was a mule driver. "This used to be a busy market town, and he led the mules all the way to Buffalo." Nick started whistling and soon we were both singing loudly.

Had a mule. Her name was Sal.

Fifteen miles on the Erie Canal.

"Wouldn't catch me dragging a barge full of cabbages on a muddy tow path," said Nick.

"He didn't do it for long. Trains and trucks took over."

Now Waterville was a two-light town, one at each end of Main Street. That consequence suited me fine.

Chapter Two
Canal Disaster

The day was hot and muggy and soon our hands and faces were berry streaked.

As we neared the bridge that crossed the Erie Canal, we looked at the inviting cool gray, green water. Come summer we always wore our swim trunks under our clothes.

"C'mon," Nick said." Let's wash off the evidence. I'll race you."

I looked at our buckets of berries. "We have to get these home. Ma's waiting."

"Ten minutes, Pete. Gee whiz. Leave'em on the grass. No one will take'em." He flung his overalls and shirt onto the tow path and ran ahead. "Hurry up, Slow Poke," he called leaping down the grassy, dirt bank. I didn't rush. What was the point? Nick won every race he ever ran.

Except the last one.

By noon I knew it would be a scorcher. But it was still cool in the shade of the maple trees. I let the breeze fan my face, and avoided all the cracks in the sidewalk. Soon the street would be filled with families and commotion from the annual July 4th parade. But at that hour it was silent.

As I neared the tow path, I saw Nicholas's shirt and overalls in a jumbled pile. "Coming," I called, as I slipped the straps of my overalls over my shoulders and pulled off the faded denim pants.

"*Help!*" the cry shot through the air from the canal below. I thought my friend was pretending to need help. I 'd told Nick not to do that. Over and over. "Suppose you were really in trouble. Or danger."

"Nothing dangerous ever happens here," he'd said with a trace of disgust. "This is Waterville. Not the jungle." But each time I foolishly rushed to the rescue, Nick would burst into a full-throated laugh, as though it was a big joke. So, this one time I didn't pay attention. The canal water wasn't really dangerous, Still, it was twelve feet deep, and an occasional boat went through.

"*Pete, Help I---.*" The rest of the sentence was broken off. His voice was different. Panicked.

I dashed over to the edge of the bank half-expecting to see Nick with a wide grin across his face. But when I looked down, I saw a huge, black dog jumping on top of Nick.

I peeled off my shirt, grabbed the fallen branch of a tree and raced down the bank.

Yelling, I jumped in the water and flung the branch as far as I could, hoping to distract the dog.

11

Nicholas' arms flailed wildly.

It looked like the dog was pushing him under water.

But when the dog saw the stick fly by, he suddenly stopped and raced after the branch instead.

Frantically, I tried to get my best friend to shore. Nicholas's face was pale and scared. He tried to swim but his legs barely moved.

"I'll have to swim for two of us," I thought, and struggled to reach the tow path. But my back was sore from picking strawberries. My muscles ached, and it was hard to carry his weight.

Suddenly, the black dog returned and jumped on both of us. I let go of Nicholas so I could push the barking animal off. "Go," I shouted to Nick. "Quick"

Then, I struggled to fight off the animal that was scratching my legs with its sharp nails, dragging me into the middle of the canal and trying to bite me. Yelling and kicking, I finally scared him off. With a low growl the black dog swam away. I couldn't stop shaking and my teeth were chattering. I didn't know how long the battle lasted. Was it two minutes or twenty? But when I looked around, I didn't see Nick. "Good," I thought. "He made it."

Exhausted, I crawled up the bank. Our clothes were still there and so were the pails of strawberries. But Nicholas wasn't.

"*NICK!*" I shouted.

There was no answer.

"*NICK!!!*"

The silence was terrifying.

"*HELP!*" I hollered, racing turning down Main Street. "Help. Quick."

But it was a holiday morning. Festivities wouldn't start until much later. Main Street was deserted.

I raced to the Sheriff's house and banged on the door.

When help finally came, it was too late.

Chapter 3
Peter

Back home I couldn't absorb the terrible news.

Nick, my best friend, gone.

Drowned.

There was only one large black dog in Waterville. Nevada. I kept wondering if the dog had followed Nick into the canal. Or was the dog already there? Why did the dog chase the stick I threw, then attack us? Troubling questions tumbled in my mind.

"We could have lost you too," Ma said, tears glistening in her eyes, as she hugged me tightly.

The doorbell rang, and I heard the Sheriff talking to my parents, but up in my room. I couldn't speak, or move, or cry. What kind of a person can't save his best friend? Was it all my fault? Worse, why this one time, didn't I run as soon as I heard Nick's cry for help?

For hours I sat on the wooden floor staring out my screened in window ignoring the heat that poured in and the voices in the street below. How could there ever be a

July 4th three-legged race without Nick? I threw my pillow across the room wanting to break something, glad when my bureau light crashed to the floor. How could there be school next fall without Nick? How could there be a world without Nick?

When my father knocked on the door, I didn't answer. Then Dad walked in and sat down beside me.

"We've been talking to the sheriff," he said. "Have you ever heard of the State Farm Market Law?"

"No," I mumbled, wishing he'd leave me alone.

"It allows for a dangerous animal to be put to death."

"Good."

My father looked me in the eye. "Peter, Mr. Price insists that it *wasn't* his dog."

"Does the sheriff believe that?" I demanded. "After what happened?"

My father wiped his brow with a handkerchief. "Bixby Price protested, Peter. Said the dog never left his side all day, refused to let the sheriff take the dog into custody until he called the Dog Society. So, to be fair---."

"Fair to who?" I shouted. "Not to Nick."

My father put a hand on my shoulder. "Let me finish, Son. The sheriff's allowing the Dog Society to observe the dog for two weeks."

"That's crazy."

"And," my dad continued after a deep sigh, "the sheriff suspects the Dog Society may demand a trial to let a judge decide." Wiping his brow again, he added, "Your mother and I hate to see you go through all that, Peter, unless you're absolutely positive."

"I was there, Dad, remember?"

"Then, come to the picnic supper. Others need to hear what you have to say."

The mood in the village square was somber. The flag was lowered to half-mast. I knew that they only did that when important people died, like presidents and heroes … and now Nick.

At the supper the minister asked for a moment of silence to remember the spirit of a once happy child. Only a few hours ago a huge dog had changed their lives.

The picnic table groaned with fried chicken, baked beans, corn bread, buttermilk biscuits, Jello salad, pitchers of lemonade, and waving above were red, white and blue streamers twisted together. I knew families had been preparing for days and weren't going to let all that food go to waste. But how can anyone eat, I thought. I wanted to tip the whole picnic table to the ground. Instead, I kicked the wooden leg as hard as I could, until Ma placed a firm hand on my knee.

She'd made my favorite, but I left my plate of fried chicken, untouched. When Ma brought out the dessert, I stood up ready to bolt from the table so no one would see my tears. Nick and I had picked those strawberries that morning, and the night before, we'd practiced with a flour sack so we'd be sure to win the annual three-legged race.

My father reached out, stopping me with an arm around my waist. In a low, gentle voice he said, "Not eating won't bring him back. "

"I know. But I can't. I can't. Not when---. He was my best friend." I started to leave but my dad stopped me.

"People need to hear what you saw."

Dad banged a large spoon on the table to get everyone's attention. His eyes blazed "We cannot have a wild animal running loose in Waterville,' There was a murmur of agreement from neighbors. "So, no matter what the Dog Society's observation finds or what Mr. Price says, my son thinks it was *his* dog that attacked them." He turned to me." Peter, tell them."

"I know it was. It was Nevada," I said my voice shaking. "I saw him. I was the only one who did. I fought him off... and then----."

But I couldn't continue. I ran down the block from the Village Green into our house and into my room. Why hadn't Nick waited for me to go swimming? I would have checked the canal both ways for boats, the way I always did, and seen the dog. I would have stopped him from jumping in. Why was Nick always in a rush, I thought in anger. I lay on the bed sobbing. What difference did it make now? Sure, I'd tried to save him, but I'd failed. I slammed my fist into the pillow wanting to start the day all over again, to erase the morning and give July 4th a happy ending. Why couldn't life be like a comic book, where the hero always wins?

Later that evening a knock came at my door. When I didn't answer Ma walked in and put down a tray of food on the edge of the bureau, sliding aside the pieces of a half-finished model airplane, my bag of marbles and the framed snapshot of me and Nicholas winning the three-legged race last year.

Ma sat down rolling the edge of her apron in her fingers. "Peter," she said, then stopped.

"It isn't fair," I whispered.

"No," she agreed. "It isn't. But there it is," she said stroking his back. "Petey, you tried to save him. You did what you could."

She hadn't called me Petey since I was little and what was odd, I didn't mind.

She gestured towards the tray. "I've left supper for you. Been saving up all summer to make your favorite." She took a handkerchief from her apron pocket and wiped her tearing eyes. "Who knew what today would bring? Try to eat some, Petey, if you can."

"You always tell me no food in the bedroom."

"Sometimes rules have to be broken," she said and kissed me gently on the top of my head.

She didn't even tell me to pick up my clothes off the floor.

But, later, I did.

And much later I ate a piece of fried chicken.

Chapter 4
News

Sensational items and bad news travel fast.

This story was both.

Telegraph wires hummed.

I stood in front of the drugstore newsstand reading the front -page headlines: "Canal tragedy," "Dog Accused," "Dog Society Demands Trial." Those words competed with the alarming news that ten pounds of potatoes now cost thirty-one cents. But what grabbed my full attention was a magazine cover showing a woman cuddling her Chihuahua. When I flipped through the pages there was a photo of her writing a check to the Dog Society. On her enclosed note she'd printed in red capital letters, "Defend the dog. Charges preposterous!"

I liked most dogs well enough, but up until that day on the canal I'd never paid much attention to Nevada.

"Got a mean streak, that dog," Nick said whenever we saw him in the distance, chasing a stick that his owner threw.

"How do you know for sure?".

Nick ran his hand through his black hair and frowned. "I dunno." He shrugged. "I just feel it."

But that didn't explain why Nevada attacked us. I thought about the problem every day. But I didn't come up with an answer.

Although disagreement raged, most Waterville citizens demanded the death of the dog. For me there was no question. There wasn't any need for a trial. The answer was simple. The dog was guilty. I ought to know. I was there.

Lawyers were appointed. Witnesses summoned and the trial was set for the first Monday in August before a judge without a jury.

Chapter 5
August

Ma put out a freshly ironed white shirt for me, long pants, one of my father's ties and a pair of new black shoes.

"I'm gonna roast," I thought, as I checked the bathroom mirror. I had the same haircut, brown hair parted on the side, but the freckles on my face looked older somehow. My mouth was set in a tight line as if it knew it would never laugh again. I threw my shoulders back, swallowed hard, and told myself, "It's for Nick."

At the last minute I grabbed my lucky marble and slipped it in my pocket. Nick gave it to me back in third grade when we swore to be best friends forever. It was a glistening white marble shot through with blues and greens. Nick said it looked like a beach beside a tropical sea. "One day we'll go find it," he said. That was when we invented our special secret handshake: both hands clapped, twisted thumbs and our left hands slapped together.

"You look very grown-up," Ma said inspecting me before we left for the Village Hall.

"I'm the key witness," I answered. But when I entered the packed courtroom and saw all the protest signs, my hands felt clammy. I wished it were two months ago and we were going out to play catch or shoot marbles.

Chapter 6
The Village Hall

Word had spread that the trial would be covered by a movie newsreel reporter and played in movie theatres across the country. Women wore their best summer dresses and hats. Some even wore white gloves. Most of the men were in summer suits. The old Village Hall had a new coat of white paint and an overhead fan droned but did little to cool the room.

I watched as the movie newsreel man set up a hand crank movie camera called a coffee grinder. The man's face was red from heat and excitement as his camera whirred taking in all the placards. "Spare Nevada's life" in big blue letters. Another read in thin menacing lines, "Mongrel is Murderer." A large banner held up by three members of the Dog Society read, "A Dog is Man's Best Friend." Two second graders, each with long braids tied in ribbons, held up a bright yellow sign that pleaded, "Tie him up, but don't shoot."

"This is Barney Wyman," the reporter said into a

microphone, "Movietone News." He introduced himself to the crowd and to all his future audiences. Then he moved to Nevada's metal cage. "And here's the dog on trial," he intoned, "Guilty or not?" He poked his camera even closer. "He's a defendant who can't speak for himself." A sharp bark came from the cage.

Barney Wyman smiled. "Or maybe he can."

Chapter 7
Lawyers

A brief silence fell as the two lawyers entered.

Suddenly, I was worried. One of them would win the case. But which one? Why did there have to be a trial anyway? It was obvious that Nevada was guilty.

Prosecuting Attorney, Bradford Kelly, wore a dark gray suit and shoes so shiny I bet he could see his face in them. The kind you don't dare get dirty. Nick would have called them Sunday Best Shoes and tossed them into the back of his closet. Bradford Kelly walked straight to a table on the left and set down his leather briefcase, which had the initials BK stamped in gold. He nodded to his adversary, the Defense Attorney, who walked towards the table on the right. "Good morning, Miss Ross. How's your client?"

"In a cage," she said tartly. She was dressed in a navy cotton dress with her hair pulled back in a tight bun. Her briefcase looked brand new. She reminded me of a little kid playing grown-up.

"You can't allow a criminal to roam around free," Mr.

Kelly said. His tone was calm, but his eyes were cold and calculating.

Andrea Ross drew all of her five feet up and glared. "In this country any man, woman, child or animal is innocent until proven guilty."

"And I," Mr. Kelly pounced back, "intend to prove that he's a killer."

The room was quiet as the spectators listened to the lawyers argue.

I agreed with Mr. Kelly, but I didn't like the way he was trying to rattle Miss Ross. Facts alone should win the case.

"Mr. Kelly," she asked, her voice icy, "Do you know what murder is?"

He laughed and so did some of the spectators. "Of course, I do," he answered. "It's killing—."

"No," she interrupted, slamming her briefcase down on the table. "It's pre-meditation upon the part of the killer. The legal definition says that it's the unlawful killing of a human with malice aforethought. So, how can you possibly determine criminal responsibility for a dog?" There were cheers from members of the Dog Society. "How can you think of blaming him for such a deed?"

"Miss Ross," said Mr. Kelly smoothly, "Will you be representing a rabbit next?"

There were loud laughs from the audience. That's mean, I thought. All he has to do is prove what's true.

I sat up straighter. That's why I was there.

Chapter 8
The Trial Begins

Morning sunlight flooded the room as Justice Jeremiah Ethan Wright in black judicial robes swept in.

"Wait," cried the news reporter. Aiming his camera, he caught the white-haired man mid-step to the judge's bench. "That's it, Justice Wright. Thanks." He introduced himself with an ingratiating smile. "Barney Wyman, Your Honor. Movietone News. Where the action is, that's where my camera is."

The judge leaned across his desk, wagging his finger. "Kindly remember this is a courtroom, Mr. Wyman. Not a movie theatre."

Barney Wyman nodded. "Yes, Your Honor. You won't even know I'm here."

"I doubt that," the judge said. "But remember the purpose of this court is to serve justice. Not popcorn."

Justice, I thought. That's exactly what I want.

The judge banged his gavel and gravely addressed the spectators in the Village Hall.

"The matter for this court today concerns the drowning of a youth, Nicholas Winters, in the canal where a large dog attacked him." At that there was a broken sob from Mrs. Winters. I saw Mr. Winters put an arm around his wife to comfort her. But his face was drawn and his shoulders stooped. I remembered Nicholas saying he didn't want a life counting cans of tuna fish. What a terrible way to have had that wish come true.

The judge cited the State Farm Market Law. I knew it meant you could put a dangerous animal to death. I looked over at the dog, resting in his cage. Did Nevada know why he was there? I shifted in my chair and wished I wasn't sitting so close.

The judge turned to the Prosecuting Attorney. "Call your first witness."

Chapter 9
Bixby Price, First Witness

Bixby Price shuffled towards the witness stand, His pants were frayed at the cuff, his old boots scuffed, and though his shirt was washed it was wrinkled. As he passed close by, I saw toast crumbs caught in his beard. Nevada barked and wagged as Mr. Price bent over the cage.

"Hello ol' fella," he said before continuing to the bench.

The judge held out a Bible instructing Mr. Price to place his left hand on its black leather cover and swear to tell the truth, the whole truth and nothing but the truth.

Then, Mr. Kelly began his interrogation with a seemingly routine question. "Where was your dog on July 4th?"

"Home. All day."

"Are you sure?" asked Mr. Kelly.

Now, the dog owner looked nervous. "He was on the porch most of the day, kinda dozing…like me. Nevada doesn't like heat."

Mr. Kelly smiled. A tricky smile, I thought. "Most of

the day," the lawyer repeated. "But not all of the day, Mr. Price?"

Bixby Price sat up straight. "A dog's a dog, Mr. Kelly."

"Precisely," answered Mr. Kelly, with another smile. "And isn't the canal a perfect place to cool off?"

Sneaky, I thought. I could see where the lawyer was going.

"Sure t'is," agreed Bixby Price, then paused. A look of suspicion crossed his face as though he sensed a trap. "But I didn't take him there that day."

"But you have at other times?"

Mr. Price nodded, then added defensively," Not a crime neither. He likes to swim with me. We're friends. Best friend I got." I saw beads of perspiration on his forehead and knew it wasn't only the heat in the room.

The lawyer rifled through his papers, then asked, "How would you describe your dog?"

"Part Airedale, part German shepherd."

"In other words, a mongrel."

Bixby Price bristled. "He is what I said."

"Would you agree that your dog is large?" Looking directly at me, he added, "Say, as big as this boy sitting here?" A room full of spectators turned to stare at me, and I could feel my face flush. "About the same size?" persisted Mr. Kelly.

"You can measure 'em both if you've a mind to," the witness snapped.

I hoped there was no such plan. But then Mr. Kelly took a different tack.

"Is your dog intelligent?" asked the Prosecuting Attorney.

At that Bixby Price lost his temper. "I reckon more than you are."

"Objection," said Bradford Kelly.

"Sustained," said Justice Wright, reminding the witness to answer the questions without additional comments.

"Is your dog intelligent?" repeated the lawyer.

At that there was a loud bark from the cage. A broad grin spread across Bixby Price's face. "Reckon that's your answer, Lawyer Kelly." The spectators laughed, and Mr. Kelly quickly covered his embarrassment by consulting his notes.

The next question stopped the laughter.

"Is that why you sent him to Obedience School last February to become a Guard Dog?"

Bixby Price was flustered. His voice lowered. I had to lean forward to hear.

"It weren't no good. He's too friendly. Only there two months."

"Long enough," countered Mr. Kelly, "to learn how to attack."

"But he doesn't," insisted Bixby Price. "Not in his nature."

"A dog's nature can change. A dog can attack without

reason." Bradford Kelly thumped his briefcase for emphasis. "It's called an aberration. A departure from the normal."

"I know what it means," said Bixby Price. He looked angry. I wondered why the lawyer had to be so mean and worried what questions the lawyer was going to ask me.

"What was the weather like on July 4th?" asked Mr. Kelly.

"You know as well as I do," answered Bixby Price, with a look of surprise. "Hot and muggy."

Mr. Kelly smiled with a glint of triumph in his eyes. "You've testified Nevada is intelligent, doesn't like heat, enjoys a swim in the canal, and went to obedience school. So, Nevada certainly could have found his way to the canal and gone for a swim, while you were dozing on your porch. To quote you, 'a dog's a dog.' That'll be all, Mr. Price". With a sweeping gesture he turned to the Defense Attorney. "Your witness."

I was amazed at the lawyer's clever use of testimony. Sweat collected around my collar as the fan ineffectively droned above me. What would happen when I took the witness stand?

Andrea Ross reaffirmed that Nevada was Mr. Price's dog and asked how long he'd had him.

Bixby Price explained," See, when I was out west, there was this litter of puppies on the ranch. But no one wanted him." He paused to blow on his spectacles and polish them against his shirt. "Dogs need friends just like us. So, I took him. Named him for the place he was born."

Some people smiled, touched by what the old man said.

"Did Nevada ever bite or claw or scratch you?" Miss Ross continued.

"He's never been a lick of trouble," asserted Bixby Price.

"Does he like children?" she asked.

"Likes to play, he does. If one of them throws a ball or a stick, he'll go fetch it. But he likes to play with me best." There was an edge of pride in his voice.

I thought about the stick I'd thrown, how the dog had rushed after it.

The Defense Attorney looked at her client and asked if he'd heard of the State Farm Market Law.

Bixby Prices' shoulders sagged. "With all this going on 'course I heard of it," he said. Then, he leaned forward. "But I can tell you Nevada is not vicious, never was, never will be." He sat back, exhausted, wiped his sweating brow, and dried his damp hands on his trousers.

"That's what I intend to prove," said Andrea Ross, glancing over at her opposition. "Mr. Kelly here thinks your dog is dangerous and should be executed."

"*NO!*" the tormented cry flew from Bixby Price and filled the courtroom. There were tears in his eyes. "He's wrong. All you have to do is look at Nevada. He's friendly, playful. Why when I come home, he jumps up, wags his tail and licks my face. Sure, he'll lick anything. But he doesn't bite. And he wouldn't hurt a young'un."

Miss Ross had a look of satisfaction as she held out a hand to help him down. "Thank you. You may step down."

"Don't you worry ol' fella," he told his dog as he passed the cage that imprisoned him. "I'm gonna fight for you."

There were sympathetic murmurs in the courtroom.

The trial was going to be harder than I thought. And I admit I felt sort of sorry for Mr. Price. No one wants to lose a best friend.

But I was here for Nick.

Chapter 10
Peter Henderson, Witness

I gulped and stood slowly. I knew that my evidence was crucial to the case.

As I put my left hand on the worn black leather Bible the judge intoned, "Do you promise to tell the truth, the whole truth and nothing but the truth?"

"Yes." My voice squeaked, but no one laughed.

The judge peered over his glasses and assured me that there was nothing to be afraid of. But what if Nevada remembered me? What if he got loose and attacked again?

"On behalf of this village," said Justice Wright, "we want to commend your bravery in trying to save Nicholas Winters."

"But it didn't help." The words burst out. "He was my best friend. Since third grade." My voice cracked.

"A grievous loss," said Justice Wright, nodding in compassion. "But we need your testimony in order to proceed."

"You're our key witness," encouraged Mr. Kelly.

I stood as tall as I could to relay the events of that July 4th morning. I wanted every person in the courtroom to care about the victim and to condemn the criminal. When I finished, Mr. Kelly said, "Can you identify the dog?"

I pointed.

The dog scratched the side of his cage and stuck his paw out. Though the room was stifling, I shivered.

"Your witness,' Mr. Kelly said, as if the matter were settled.

Andrea Ross approached Peter and spoke gently. "No one in this courtroom questions your courage or loyalty to your friend. But in such an emotional moment, it's possible to make a mistake."

She turned to the judge. "Your Honor, may I introduce some unusual evidence that bears directly on the case?"

He nodded and at her signal another huge cage was brought into the courtroom.

Peter stared, stunned.

There was an outburst of shocked surprise from the spectators, who strained to see the second dog behind the wire mesh.

"Peter," continued the Defense Attorney, "I'd like you to compare these two dogs. Tell us if you see any resemblance."

When I approached the two cages, side by side, both dogs growled.

I stepped back in a hurry.

"What do you see?" she asked.

"They're both large. They both have black hair and they each have a white patch between the ears." It was so still in the court room that I was sure everyone could hear my heart hammering. Throwing my shoulders back I ventured a few steps closer. "But that other dog, this new one...I've never seen him."

"No," agreed the Defense Attorney. "Leroy lives three towns away. But isn't it possible he might have wandered here, plunged into the canal to cool off, seen a strange boy dive in, wanted to play and in so doing jumped on the boy? Or for that matter, it might have been a completely different dog."

"Objection," shouted the Prosecuting Attorney. "The witness has already identified the murderer as Nevada."

Miss Ross looked at him coldly. "Not to my satisfaction."

With a thwack of his gavel the judge declared, "Objection overruled."

I looked at the two lawyers, the judge, the dogs, the room full of spectators all watching, waiting for me to speak. In the silence Mrs. Winters sobbed. At that moment I would have gladly been anywhere but the Village Hall.

"All I know," I said in a loud, firm voice, "is that my best friend was killed." I pointed to Nevada. "And that's the dog that did it."

As I was excused, I raced out of the room before

37

anyone could see the tears fall uncontrollably down my face.

A moment later, my father stood beside me in the white walled hallway, which was hung with solemn portraits of past local dignitaries. My grandfather, great- grandfather and great-great grandfather looked down on us. Putting an arm around me, my father said, "Pete, you did what you had to do."

"Won't bring Nick back," I mumbled into dad's shoulder.

"But those two dogs looked an awful lot alike," my father mused. He lifted my chin and looked into my eyes. "Are you sure, son?"

And then I had a terrible thought. What if Nevada wasn't guilty? All I'd actually seen was a large, black dog thrashing in the water.

"It's easy to be confused, when you're upset," Dad said.

Nodding, I remembered the night, right after Grandma died, that we'd hunted all over the house for the keys my mother lost. Ma was adamant she'd brought them inside. So, we searched the kitchen, the living room, the dining room. The next morning I found them. Outside.

"Dad," I hesitated. "What if I made a mistake?"

He looked at me with a slight frown and glanced at the portraits of the steely-eyed forefathers hanging above. "No matter how you feel, Peter, it's your moral obligation to tell the truth." Dad started to walk back to the courtroom, then turned and put a firm hand on my shoulder. "A hasty decision without sufficient evidence, Peter, condemns the innocent, not the guilty. It's crucial that you're certain."

Chapter 11
Diana Storey, Witness

When I returned to the courtroom, I groaned. There was Diana Storey on the stand. There was no telling what a girl who wanted attention would say.

She was boasting that she was a Girl Scout and always told the truth. What's more she'd sold more Girl Scout cookies than anyone.

There was a titter of laughter in the room. The Prosecuting Attorney looked annoyed.

"Do you have a good memory?" the Prosecuting Attorney asked.

"I know all the capitols of all forty-eight states. Do you want me to recite them?"

"No," boomed Bradford Kelly. "Just answer the questions, please. Where were you on the morning of July 4th?"

"See, it was a holiday," Diana began.

Everyone knows that, I thought, disgusted.

"I went out to play but there wasn't anyone around, so

I decided to follow my brother."

Boy, was glad I didn't have a little sister.

Impatient, Lawyer Kelley persisted. "Did you go to the canal?"

"First, I hid behind the trees and rubbish barrels. And he never ever saw me. See, I'm going to be a detective, when I grow up," Diana chattered on. "This library book I read said the most important thing is 'how to observe and remember details.' So, I was practicing. When I climbed up a tree, I could see far away. That's when I saw a big black dog on the road headed for the canal. He wasn't coming from Mr. Price's house either. That's why I'm sure it wasn't Nevada and----."

"Could you tell the court the title of that detective book you read," Bradford Kelly interrupted.

"*Famous Detectives and Famous Crimes.* It's a big green book. Nearly 500 pages." With a toss of her pigtails, adorned in white ribbons, she added, "And I read it all in one week."

Bradford Kelly sighed heavily. "That's fine, Diana, but the correct title is *Famous Crimes, Famous Detectives.*"

"Oh," Diana paused, then shrugged. "That's almost the same."

"Almost," thundered the Prosecuting Attorney, "but not exactly. Between 'almost' and 'exactly,' Diana, is the difference between being slipshod and being accurate. That's a very important difference for a would-be detective or for a witness in court. Keep that in mind before you

41

blurt out whatever pops into your head."

Andrea Ross bolted up. "Objection, Your Honor. Neither the library book nor the witness is on trial."

The judge smothered the hint of a smile. "Objection sustained."

Mr. Kelly was right, I thought, but, heck, Diana's just a kid. She looked ready to cry.

"Diana," the judge said kindly, "it's important that you only tell us what you saw. If you don't know the answer to a question, simply say, 'I don't know.' No one will be angry."

"I'm trying to tell the truth," said Diana, "as best I can."

"Proceed, Mr. Kelly," ordered the judge, "but kindly remember that the witness is a minor and is not a criminal."

"I will, Your Honor," promised the Prosecuting Attorney. But I could see from the lawyer's pinched expression that he was highly irritated.

He crossed to Nevada's cage. The dog, which had been dozing, woke and barked at him. With a frown, he backed away and pointed, "Diana, is this the animal that you saw?"

Diana crossed to the cage, bent down and whispered, "Hello, Nevada." Then she reached her finger in.

There was an audible gasp from the audience.

Nevada licked it.

No," she said confidently.

The Prosecuting Attorney crossed to the other cage.

Leroy let out a menacing growl. The lawyer stepped away fast. "Then, is this the dog you saw on the road?"

Diana studied Leroy. Her face crumpled. "I…..I." She looked at the judge. "I don't know," she said. "All I do know is that it wasn't Nevada."

Bradford Kelly sighed and led her back "Your witness, Miss Ross."

The Defense Attorney smoothed her skirt as she stood.

"How well did you know Nicholas?" she asked.

"He played baseball with my brother and sometimes they traded comic books." Instantly, Diana covered her mouth and looked nervously over at her mother. 'Not too often, because they weren't supposed to read comics on account of they're not good for you, but---."

People in the courtroom smiled.

"It's all right, Diana," said Andrea Ross. The question is were *you* friends with him?"

"'Course not," said Diana with a toss of her pigtails. "He's a boy!"

There was loud laughter at her response. Diana looked confused and said quickly,

"But I'm sorry about what happened. Really sorry."

"How often have you seen Nevada?" queried the lawyer.

"Lots of times," came the prompt reply.

"Well then, Detective Storey," said Andrea Ross, dark

43

eyes smiling. "Describe him."

"Large, black hair with a small white patch between his ears. And he licks your hand if you pet him. He's real friendly."

Maybe to you, I thought. Not to Nick. Not to me.

"Could you use your skills as a detective and look at the other dog again?" said Andrea Ross.

I could tell as she strode over to the cages that she was pleased to be called a detective. She inspected both dogs and peered at Leroy. "He sure looks a lot like Nevada."

"Yes, that my point," said the lawyer.

Diana's eyes brightened. "Do you think it's a case of mistaken identity?" she asked.

"It's possible. Do you think Leroy might have been the dog you saw headed for the canal?"

I sunk lower in my chair worried about this abrupt turn in the trial.

So was Mr. Kelly. He jumped up waving his legal papers. "Objection. The Defense Attorney is leading the witness."

There was another bang of the wooden gavel as the judge said, "Objection sustained."

"Sorry, Your Honor," Andrea Ross apologized. "One last question, Diana, did you ever see Nevada attack anyone? Or bite a child?"

At that there was a loud bark from Nevada's cage that sounded suspiciously like, "No."

"See," Diana declared. "Even Nevada said, 'No.'" She beamed as she went back to her seat.

Show-off, I thought.

But I had to admit those two dogs looked an awful lot alike.

Chapter 12
Mrs. Alma Winters, Witness

Alma Winters, dressed in mourning black from head to toe, faltered on her way to the witness stand. She looked as if a gust of wind could blow her over, as though only the cameo brooch at her throat held her together.

"Good morning, Mrs. Winters," the judge said gently, as he swore her in.

"Good morning, Justice Wright," she answered softly, fiddling nervously with her brooch as she sat down.

"We'll try to make this as brief as possible," Bradford Kelly assured her. "We are all aware of your grief."

She nodded gratefully.

"Nicholas was a fine, high-spirited lad," the judge said.

"Thank you, Justice Wright." Her voice caught. "Yes, yes, he was."

I realized that her pain must be dreadful. Probably, worse than mine.

As calmly as he could, Mr. Kelly asked, "Can you think back on that day?"

"I'll never forget it," she blurted out. "It's with me constantly."

When I looked at the caged dog, I remembered how it pushed us both down and Nick's scared face as he tried to swim.

In a surprisingly gentle tone the Prosecuting Attorney asked her to tell the court what happened.

She nodded, brushed a stray hair back and began. "I was in the kitchen. I'd just taken the buttermilk biscuits out of the oven and set them on a rack to cool. When he smelled the biscuits, he said, 'Can I have one, Mom?' and reached out his hand. But I said, 'Later, Nick. They're for the picnic.' As soon as I went down to the cellar to get some apple jelly for the biscuits, I heard the screen door shut. When I came back up, he was gone. That was the last thing I ever said to him." Her shoulders were shaking, and she swallowed as she tried not to cry. "I wish I'd let him have that biscuit."

Gently, Mr. Kelly continued. "How did you learn about..." he hesitated and then said simply, "what happened?"

"It was the Sheriff," she answered in a tight voice. "He told me about ...about....." She stopped short and shuddered. "There's only one dog in the village that fits the description. Nevada."

"Is it your opinion," said the Prosecuting Attorney, "that the dog Nevada is dangerous and should be put to death?"

Yes," she said, her voice became strong and forceful. "*YES!* I know killing that dog can't bring Nick back. But it will protect the lives of other children ...and other mothers." She paused to compose herself, then rose from the wooden chair on the witness stand to demand, "Do the people of Waterville sincerely place the life of a mongrel dog above the life of a happy, healthy child?"

There was a burst of applause from local citizens.

How could anyone doubt the outcome of the trial now I thought. The torment had to end soon.

"Do you wish to question the witness," Mr. Kelly asked his adversary, more a matter of form than anything else.

But to my surprise, she said, "Yes, I do."

"Mrs. Winters, 'said the Defense Attorney. "There are two dogs here. Which one is Nevada?"

"Objection," said Bradford Kelly. "Your Honor, is this necessary? Hasn't Mrs. Winters suffered enough? Does she have to face the killer?"

"It`s all right," said Alma Winters, walking over to the area where the two cages sat. "I want to get this finished." She pointed to Nevada first. Then, visibly confused, she pointed to Leroy. Troubled, she shook her head and pointed back to Nevada. "That one...I think." Puzzled, she added, "It's hard to tell. They look so much alike."

Surprised, Andrea Ross asked, "You're not positive?"

48

"I never saw the dog up close 'til now," she admitted.

"Mrs. Winters," Andrea Ross said, "How can you identify a dog, if you are not absolutely certain?"

"I'm sure of one thing, Miss Ross," said his mother. "Nicky is gone."

I wanted to rush up and take Mrs. Winters away from the dogs and the court room. She looked ready to collapse. I glanced up at the clock on the wall with its black Roman numerals on the ivory face. Four and a half hours had gone by. Women were fanning themselves and men mopping their foreheads. I knew Nick could never have sat still this long. Looking through the window I half-expected to see him jump laughing from the branch of a nearby apple tree.

One day last February there was a huge blizzard so school had to close. But as soon as it cleared, Nick knocked on my door. Whooping and hollering, we built a snow fort. Then other neighborhood kids came out and we all had a grand snowball fight. I knew from now on "snow days" would never be the same.

Squirming in my seat I looked again at the clock. The trial was taking forever.

"No one disputes the tragedy that's happened to you or how traumatic it's been," continued the Defense Attorney leading Alma Winters back to the witness stand. "But my job is to protect the innocent."

Mrs. Winters' eyes flashed. "Wasn't Nicky innocent?"

Of course, I thought. He was fun and fearless. But

49

that dog had spooked him. My hands curled in tight fists. Last winter Nick saved me from falling into a wintry canal. But come summer I couldn't save him from drowning.

Reliving that day was a nightmare.

"Since you can't identify the dog accused," said Andrea Ross to the witness, "I must ask one final question. "Was your son a strong swimmer?"

Alma Winters drew herself up indignantly. "He's a very good swimmer." There was a choked sob. "*WAS*. He was a very good swimmer." Tears fell down her face.

"The witness is excused," said Justice Wright. Andrea Ross nodded and escorted her back to her seat, where her husband offered his handkerchief. I couldn't hear the exact words he said, but the tone was soothing. Finally, the sobbing stopped and she composed herself.

Peter remembered the half-buttermilk biscuit Nick handed him that morning. Still warm. Would she feel better if she knew?

Chapter 13
Millicent Read, Last Witness

The last witness called was Millicent Read, a hefty woman in a lavender suit and matching hat that perched on top of her short gray hair. The veterinarian wore no-nonsense sensible shoes and was Executive Secretary of the Dog Society.

After she'd been sworn in, Mr. Kelley asked if in her fifteen years as a veterinarian she'd ever found a vicious dog.

She laughed as though the question was absurd. "Of course, Mr. Kelly."

I watched carefully as the Prosecuting Attorney moved in closer.

"And isn't it true that a seemingly friendly dog can suddenly attack someone?"

She paused. "It is *possible*," she said stressing the word, "but only with sufficient provocation."

"Such as?" prodded Mr. Kelly.

She thought for a moment. "If the dog were teased, mistreated or simply defending itself."

"Miss Read," said Mr. Kelly, sounding casual, "If a

dog were, let's say swimming, and got tired, what would it do?"

"Why, what any of us would do." she answered. "Get out of the water." There was laughter in the courtroom, and she looked pleased.

But I figured this wasn't an idle question. It led to the next one.

"Let's say that the bank was steep," continued the Prosecuting Attorney in the same conversational tone, "like the Barge Canal. Is it possible that the dog might get frightened and look for something to hang onto?"

"Certainly," she said with a shrug, as though the question was a silly one. "But surely you realize a child wouldn't be strong enough to support a large dog." She waved her hand dismissively. "A child would be pushed under."

"Precisely," said Bradford Kelly. "Thank you Miss Read. You've been very helpful."

I looked at the lawyer with new admiration, but I could tell Miss Read was furious.

She rose out of her chair, shaking her fist at the lawyer. "He's not a killer, and the Dog Society and I will make every effort to spare his life."

Bradford Kelly ignored her. "Your witness," he said to Andrea Ross with a dismissive wave of his hand.

I could see the Defense Attorney's worried frown. Then she half-smiled as she took a folder from her briefcase.

The trial was nearly over, but one thought kept nagging me. While I was thrashing in the water, panicked, trying to help Nick, trying to escape myself, how close did I really see the dog? All I knew was its size and the color of its fur. That's all.

Lawyer Ross asked Miss Read for an estimate of how many dogs she'd examined in the past fifteen years.

"Ten thousand," she answered with pride stressing that it was she who'd demanded that the case be adjourned until she could observe Nevada - both on land and in water. Movietone News filmed the excited cheer that rose up in a roar from the dog lovers in the room.

Andrea Ross gestured to the two cages. "Can you identify which one is Nevada."

With a sure stride the veterinarian crossed to the metal cages, looked at both and reached in to pat Nevada's head. "Here he is." He wagged his tail as though greeting an old friend.

By now my palms were sweating. What was the Defense Attorney proving? I slumped in my chair and ran my fingers around my neck wanting to loosen my tie. A disapproving look from my mother made me sit up straight.

When Miss Ross asked the veterinarian to describe Nevada's disposition, the answer was prompt. "Loveable."

"Like I told you," cried Bixby Price. "He's friendly to everyone."

Justice Wright looked over sternly.

"Did he ever bite you?" the lawyer asked the witness.

"No. He slept at the foot of my bed."

"Is he dangerous?" Andrea Ross persisted.

"If he were," Millicent Read said sharply, "you can be sure I would not have kept him at the foot of my bed."

At that the spectators laughed heartily.

But Peter chewed on his thumb as the Defense Attorney asked, "Is it your professional opinion that Nevada should be killed as a vicious dog under the State Farm Market Law?"

"I most emphatically do not," stated Millicent Read.

There were cheers and boos from the audience followed by the loud sound of the judge's gavel.

"If I thought for a minute there was any danger to any child," clarified Millicent Read, "I would be the first to condemn him. But after observing him for two weeks in every conceivable situation, I am convinced he is neither vicious nor dangerous."

Bixby Price cheered. "I told you so. I told you so."

"Mr. Price, please," said the judge.

I clenched my fist as I squirmed on the hard wooden seat. Was I wrong?

Had I made a dreadful mistake?

Chapter 14
Doubt

Jeremiah Ethan Wright called for a summation.

Barney Wyman rolled his camera closer.

"I'll be brief," said the Prosecuting Attorney as though the matter were already settled.

I knew that I should be glad that Mr. Kelly had argued a strong case, but somehow I was troubled. Nevada could be innocent. All I'd actually seen was his head and legs thrashing in the water. I'd felt the animal's heavy weight pushing us down. But both of these dogs in the courtroom were roughly the same size. I never saw the whole dog. So, what made me so sure that it was Nevada? I chewed on my thumb again.

No matter what the judge decided, one thing was certain. Nick would never come back.

I squeezed the marble in my pocket remembering the fun they'd had the day they'd invented their special secret handshake, both hands clapped, twisted thumbs and our left hands slapped together.

"If that dog is left alive," said Bradford Kelly in a voice that began softly, then rose dramatically, "he's a threat to children everywhere in this town. My key witness, Peter Henderson, testified that Nicholas Winters was drowned," he paused for effect, then continued, "by the caged dog that now sits in front of you." He pointed and shouted, "NEVADA."

I looked at my dad and remembered his words. "A hasty decision without sufficient evidence condemns the innocent, Peter, not the guilty. It's crucial that you're certain."

Bradford Kelly roared on. "Whether it was by accident or not doesn't matter. Whether the dog was being playful or vicious is no longer relevant. Nevada is dangerous and should be killed."

Alma Winters applauded and her husband shook his head in agreement.

I stared as the ceiling fan. What should I do? What if it really *was* some other dog, not Nevada? Didn't that make me guilty too? In all the confusion did I make a mistake?

The Defense Attorney's words interrupted my troubled thoughts.

"My client, Your Honor, is a dog, and I don't for a minute contend that a dog's life matches that of a child."

"Yes, it does," a voice shouted from the back of the room. As heads turned a tiny white-haired woman in a flowered dress yanked off her summer straw hat and waved it so wildly a red ribbon fell to the floor.

"Madam," the judge reprimanded her with a sharp bang of his gavel. "This is a court of law."

"Where justice should reign," she pronounced before sitting down to cheers from members of the Dog Society.

Flustered, Miss Ross continued. "I have the greatest respect for the feelings of Mrs. Winters, and I don't want anyone to misunderstand my point of view. But I also have respect for the feelings of Mr. Price. Although we've heard a great deal of testimony, no one has satisfactorily proved that Nevada is the same dog that jumped into the canal on that fateful day."

She's right I thought with a sinking stomach. That morning, I'd been sure. By afternoon, I wasn't. Should I retract my testimony, the oath I swore in court? Sworn on the Bible.

Andrea Ross turned toward the spectators and with wide open arms appealed to them. "Isn't it absurd to put a creature that can't defend itself on trial? Ladies and gentlemen, we are dealing with an accident, a tragic accident, but NOT murder. Clearly, the dog is not guilty of the charge. Plus, there is insufficient evidence to warrant penalty, punishment or destruction of Nevada."

There were wild cheers and applause from members of the Dog Society.

Alma Winters whirled on the judge. "If you let that dog go loose, he'll kill someone else's child, sure as I'm sitting here."

She muttered, "If I had a gun I'd shoot that dog myself." In despair she covered her face.

"Your Honor," said Bradford Kelly, "we should respect the feelings of the bereaved."

Justice Wright nodded. "The court excuses you, Mrs. Winters."

"No," she said tearfully. "I have to stay...for Nicky."

Barney Wyman moved his camera in closer to catch the drama, but the judge stopped him with a curt reminder. "Mr. Wyman, this is a trial, not a movie matinee."

I could see the frustration in the reporter's face, as he took one last picture of the weeping mother and then rolled the camera back.

I was torn. Nick was my best friend. But the Defense Attorney had argued well. So had the Prosecuting Attorney. With a sinking sensation I knew what my decision had to be.

Trembling, I raised my hand. The whole courtroom of townspeople and visitors stared as the judge recognized me

"Yes, Peter?"

Nervously, I stood. " I'm….I'm… that is," I stumbled, "I'm not sure anymore. I'm not positive that it was Nevada."

"Objection," cried Bradford Kelly.

"Overruled," said the judge.

I saw the astonished expressions on people's faces.

In the stunned silence that followed, the loudest sound

in the room was the overhead paddle fan. "There'll be a short recess," announced Justice Wright, as he rose from the judge's bench, his black robe sailing behind him, and left the court room.

Instantly, arguments erupted. Angry voices shouted at me. The President of the Dog Society came over to thank me and shook my hand. The Prosecuting Attorney glared at me. Men straightened their ties and women adjusted their hats as Barney Wyman filmed them and asked what they thought would happen next. Amidst all the confusion Mrs. Winters wept uncontrollably.

"Dad, did I do the right thing?"

My father placed his large hand on my shaking shoulders. "Yes," he said. "If there was any doubt. Any doubt at all. You did what was right, Son. I'm proud of you." He paused. "I'm sure it wasn't easy."

"It wasn't." I said in a low voice.

The courtroom hushed as Justice Wright strode in and took his seat. He adjusted his glasses over his ears and looked out at the assembled anxious faces. Although he had the attention of the entire room, he banged his gavel three times before announcing his decision.

"After listening to both sides, I do not consider the evidence offered by the Prosecuting Attorney sufficient to condemn this dog to death. However, a lad of this village died."

"That's right," cried Mrs. Winters.

"In fairness to all," said the judge, raising his voice," I hereby order Nevada's life be spared."

There were loud cheers and equally loud boos from the crowded courtroom.

Nevada vigorously thumped the sides of his cage with his tail.

"You can't," sobbed Mrs. Winters. "You can't."

Bradford Kelly scowled angrily. Andrea Ross smiled into the reporter's camera.

"On the express condition," said the judge in a loud voice to top the commotion, "that the dog, when not at home, be kept on a leash at all times, accompanied by his owner."

Bixby Price shook his head sadly. "All right," he agreed, His shoulder slumped

"If after two years there's no sign of trouble, Nevada will be free." Jeremiah Ethan Wright banged his gavel for the last time. "This court is adjourned."

Once again there were cheers and boos. The reporter scurried around the room to film reactions to the judge's words.

I took a deep breath and let it out in a rush. It was over. The case was settled. Finally. I knew it must have been hard for the judge, as hard as it was for *me* to stand up and change my sworn testimony.

Later, back home I held the snapshot from last July 4th, when Nick and I won the three-legged race. We were laughing as though nothing could be more fun, as though nothing could ever separate us.

"I don't know how you'd feel," I said to the grinning boy in the photograph. "But I had to be honest. I wasn't certain any longer if the dog in the canal *was* Nevada. That look-alike dog confused me. Completely. So, in the end, Justice Wright judged 'insufficient evidence.' I hope you understand, Nick. I miss you. Something awful."

Then I took the framed photo and solemnly placed it on my bookcase right beside the lucky tiger marble that Nick gave me--always to be treasured, always to be remembered.

End

"Dog on Trial"
Glossary

Aberration: A deviation from what is normal

Defense attorney: The lawyer who defends the one accused

Mistaken identity: To make an error in identification caused by a lack of skilled, careful observation

Mongrel: A dog of mixed or indeterminate breed

Premeditation: The act of thinking out a precise plan before acting upon it

Prosecuting attorney: The lawyer who prosecutes the one accused

Testimony: Responses to questioning in order to establish facts

Discussion Questions

1. What do you think points to Nevada's innocence? (You might refer to the testimony from the owner, the veterinarian, Diana, and the surprise appearance of a look-alike dog.)

2. What do you think points to Nevada's guilt? (You might refer to what the prosecuting attorney made the owner admit, the testimony from Peter and Mrs. Winters, the concept that any animal can have an aberration.)

3. This trial did not have a jury but had there been one and you were appointed one of the jurors, how would you vote?

4. Do you think that an owner is responsible for a pet's actions?

5. Which do you think is more important: the safety of the community or the rights of an individual or animal? How do you determine what is a danger to the community?

6. What are the obligations of a witness, of a juror, of a judge?

7. What is an individual's responsibility in making a decision that will impact the life of another?

8. What are some of your thoughts on the value of human life or animal life or of any form of life found in nature?

Also by Author

A Night of Tamales and Roses

Angel in the Night

Blue Toboggan

Bravo, Benny,

Christabel and the Amazing Pedal Power Challenge

Circus Home

For the Glory

Kimchi Kid

Mean to Be Free

Ms. Courageous: Women of Science

Oh, Little Ham of Buffalo, a Koran Adoption Memoir

Remember My Name

Secrets

Seven Sound and Motion Stories

Sunday Gold

Tall Boy's Journey

The Blue Jeans Rebellion

The Dragon Hammer and the Tale of Oniroku,

The Great American Train Ride

The Ice Wolf

The Last Baron of Arizona

The Shaggy Dog Murder Trial

Vasalisa